MW00900018

Dedicated to our Mom and Dad and Mama and Papa; for all your loving guidance. We are blessed to have you for parents. To our angel investors who believed in us and our dreams to create magical wonders for children. To the children of the world who will uplift their hearts & souls with books that "we wish we had when we were kids." To my lifelong friend Sasha. And to Bob Stevens; you're awesome "dude!"

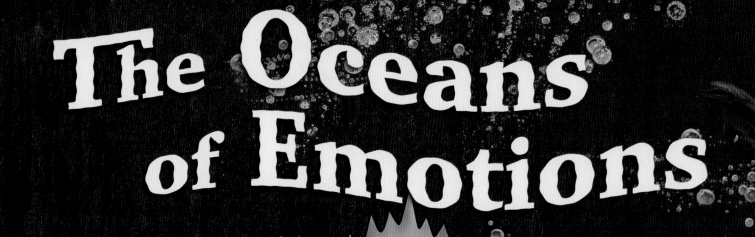

The Oceans of Emotions

Nicole K. Clark and **John T. Clark**

Illustrated by John T. Clark

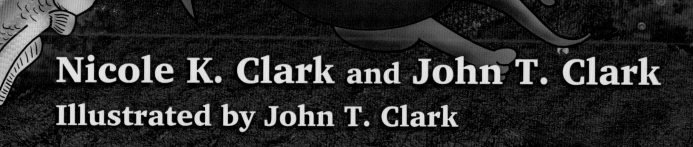

PremaNations Publishing
Uplifting Young Hearts and Minds

Once upon a time a young dragon named Destiny was on a sailing ship voyaging home from across the ocean. Her mother and father would be waiting for her when she arrived, and she was very excited to see them.

Destiny could almost see the shores of her home when a terrible storm arose and blew the ship far out to sea.

Huge waves crashed over the ship's deck and wind tore through the sails. Suddenly a great, rushing wave washed Destiny overboard into the stormy water.

Soon the storm had passed and Destiny was left alone. She tried to fly, but her wings were very sore. She called for help, but there was no one to hear her.

She began to cry and cry until she fell into a deep dragon sleep.

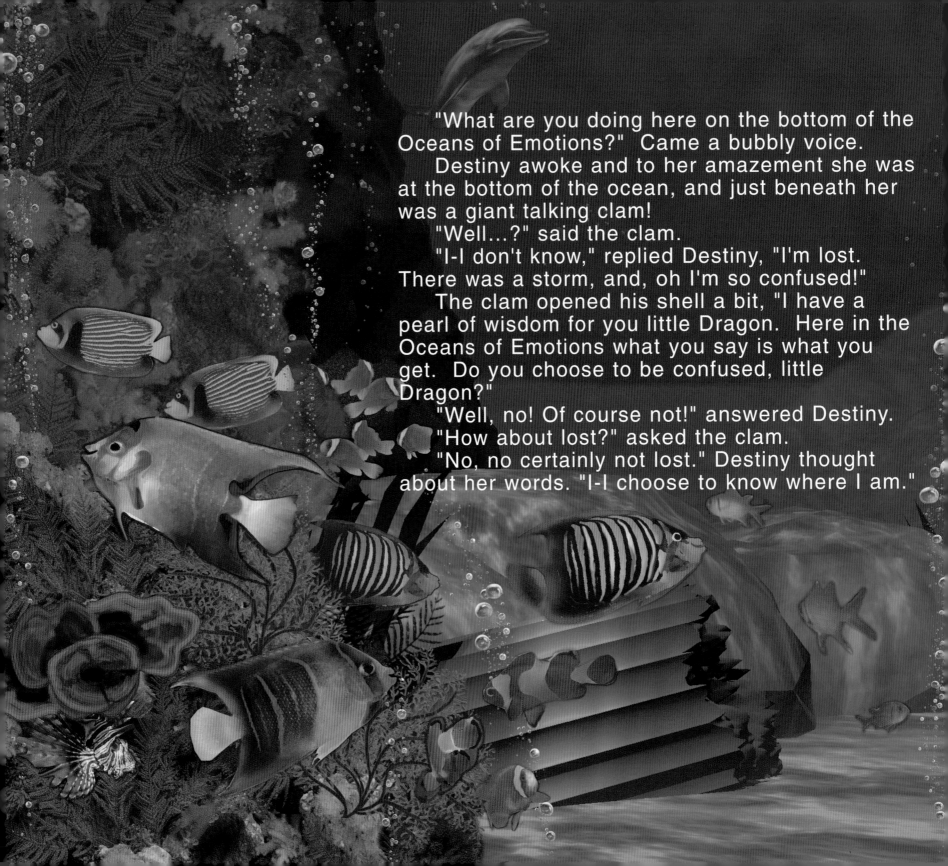

"What are you doing here on the bottom of the Oceans of Emotions?" Came a bubbly voice.

Destiny awoke and to her amazement she was at the bottom of the ocean, and just beneath her was a giant talking clam!

"Well...?" said the clam.

"I-I don't know," replied Destiny, "I'm lost. There was a storm, and, oh I'm so confused!"

The clam opened his shell a bit, "I have a pearl of wisdom for you little Dragon. Here in the Oceans of Emotions what you say is what you get. Do you choose to be confused, little Dragon?"

"Well, no! Of course not!" answered Destiny.

"How about lost?" asked the clam.

"No, no certainly not lost." Destiny thought about her words. "I-I choose to know where I am."

"A good choice!" bubbled the clam. "You're at the bottom of the Oceans of Emotions, my name is Calamity. Where are you going, Dragon?"

Destiny thought for a moment, "I'm going home! I was washed overboard in a terrible storm and I have to find my way home."

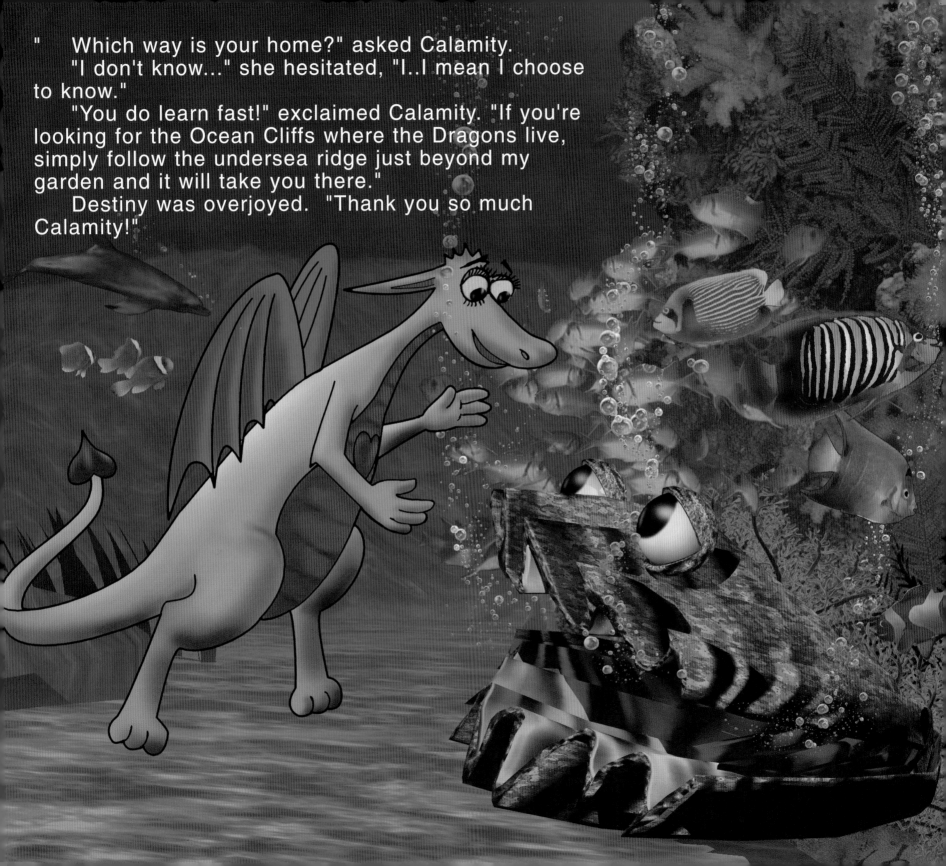

"   Which way is your home?" asked Calamity.

"I don't know..." she hesitated, "I..I mean I choose to know."

"You do learn fast!" exclaimed Calamity. "If you're looking for the Ocean Cliffs where the Dragons live, simply follow the undersea ridge just beyond my garden and it will take you there."

Destiny was overjoyed. "Thank you so much Calamity!"

Destiny found the ridge rising from the ocean bottom, yet she had entered a strong underwater current and was swimming ahead very slowly.
    As the current grew stronger Destiny had to swim faster and faster. Her arms and legs began to ache. "I can't go on," she moaned, "This is so hard! I'm so tired!"

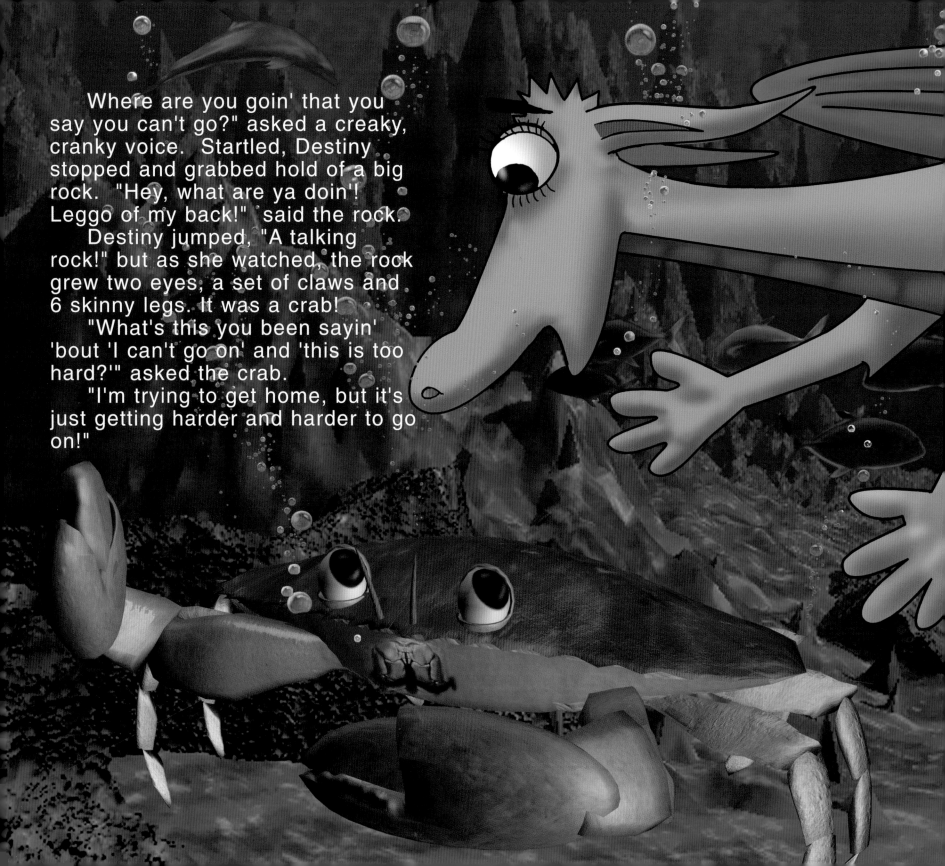

Where are you goin' that you say you can't go?" asked a creaky, cranky voice. Startled, Destiny stopped and grabbed hold of a big rock. "Hey, what are ya doin'! Leggo of my back!" said the rock.

Destiny jumped, "A talking rock!" but as she watched, the rock grew two eyes, a set of claws and 6 skinny legs. It was a crab!

"What's this you been sayin' 'bout 'I can't go on' and 'this is too hard?'" asked the crab.

"I'm trying to get home, but it's just getting harder and harder to go on!"

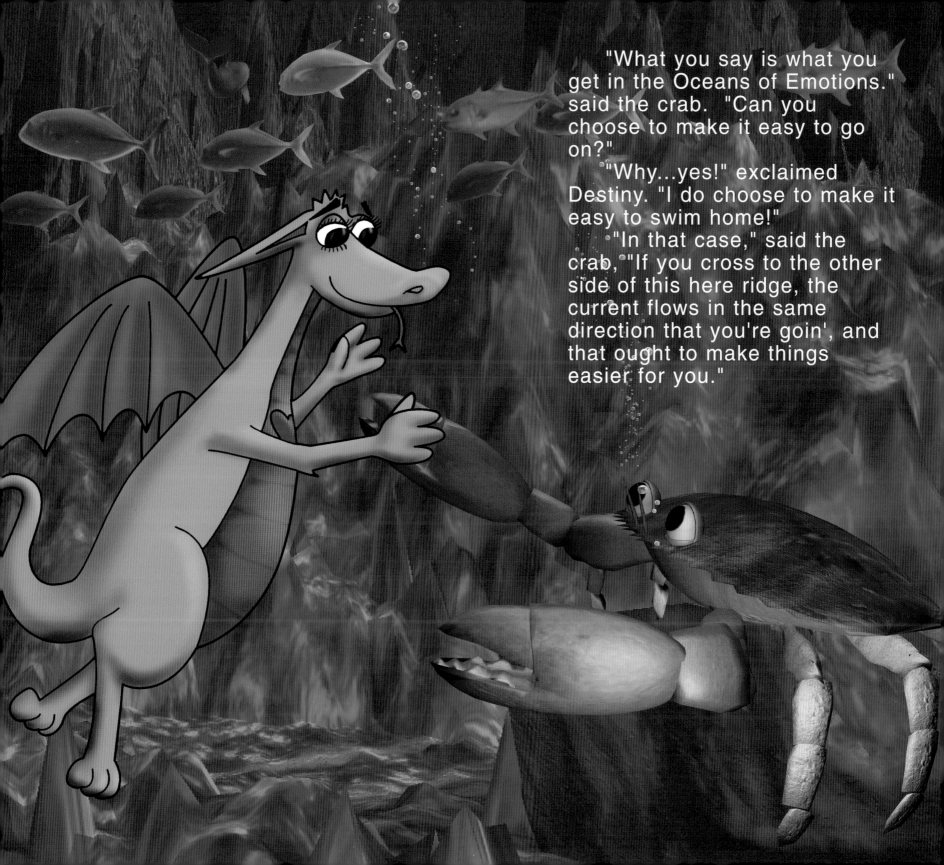

"What you say is what you get in the Oceans of Emotions." said the crab. "Can you choose to make it easy to go on?"

"Why...yes!" exclaimed Destiny. "I do choose to make it easy to swim home!"

"In that case," said the crab, "If you cross to the other side of this here ridge, the current flows in the same direction that you're goin', and that ought to make things easier for you."

Crab showed Destiny a dark tunnel that would take her to the other side of the ridge.

Destiny was deep inside the tunnel when a sudden rush of water sent her spinning in circles until she was lost.

"Oh, no! Which way do I go? Oh, this is horrible!" She put her hands over her face and began to cry, "I'll never find my way home," she sobbed, "I'll never see my Mom and Dad again."

In the darkness, Griefy Grouper could hear Destiny crying. "What are you feeling sad about little Dragon?" he asked.

"I-I'm lost and I want to go home," she sniffled.

"Well it sounds like you are almost there," responded Griefy Grouper.

"Really? How do you know?" Destiny asked.

"Because your sadness is your joy returning, little Dragon. If you make it okay to feel sad, then your tears will become tears of joy."

"Look Destiny, can you see the light?" asked Griefy Grouper.

Destiny looked down the dark passage, "Yes, yes I can see light. But is that my way?"

Grouper looked into Destiny's eyes, "Ask your heart, little Dragon."

Destiny closed her eyes and asked her heart, "Is this my way home?" Her heart warmed and she felt great joy and excitement flow through her. She had found her way home. Destiny waved to the grouper as she continued.

On and on the current carried Destiny toward her home, but when the water suddenly became much darker and deeper she began to worry, "Am I going the wrong way? What if I've been going the wrong way all this time?" She stopped and looked around, but all she could see was dark, empty water. "Oh, where do I go? Somebody help me!" she called.

"Hey! Are you feeling AFRAID?" asked a little voice.
Destiny spun around, "What? Who?..."
"I said, it sounds like you're feeling fear!" Swimming right up
to Destiny's green dragon nose was a colorful little minnow.

"What do you mean? I-I'm not afraid." answered Destiny.
"Oh, yes you are!" insisted Minnow.
Destiny gave in, "Well, okay, I was feeling a little worried."
Just a little?" asked Minnow.

"Okay, Minnow! I was feeling afraid! Who made you the expert on fear anyway?"
The Minnow darted around her head, "Just look at me! I'm everybody's lunch.
Every day I swim through the Oceans of Emotions with bigger fish ready to gobble me
up at any moment. Now that's something to feel afraid of. Yet by facing and
embracing my fears I have found real faith and courage. Now I am really living!"

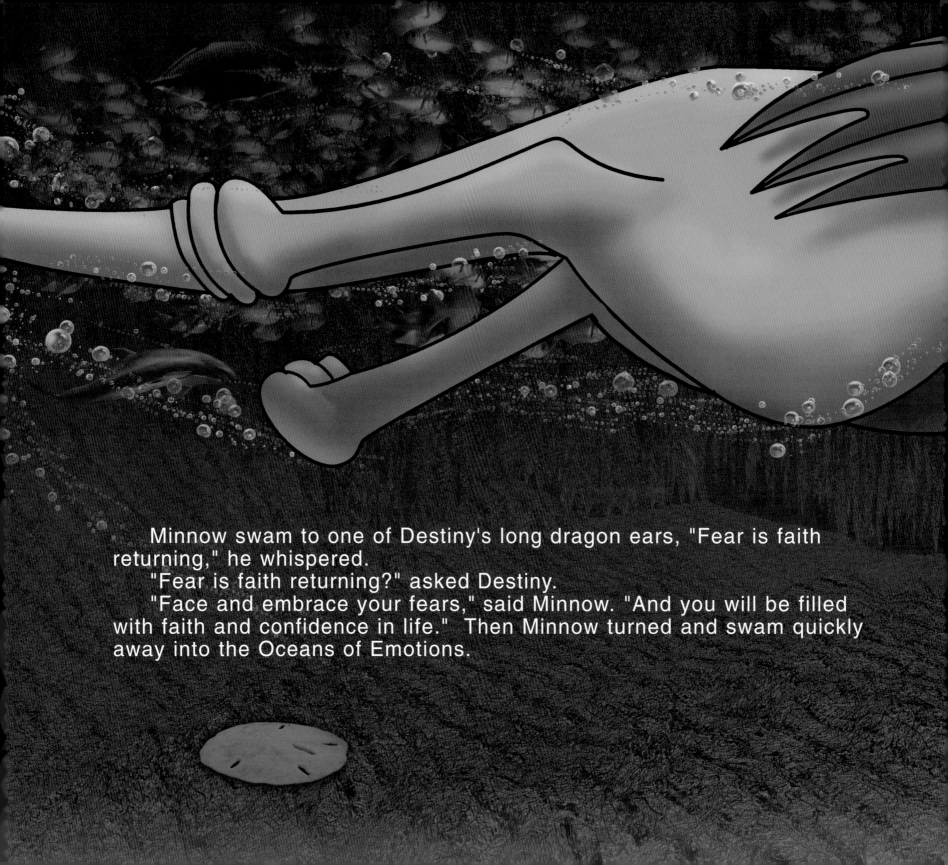

Minnow swam to one of Destiny's long dragon ears, "Fear is faith returning," he whispered.

"Fear is faith returning?" asked Destiny.

"Face and embrace your fears," said Minnow. "And you will be filled with faith and confidence in life." Then Minnow turned and swam quickly away into the Oceans of Emotions.

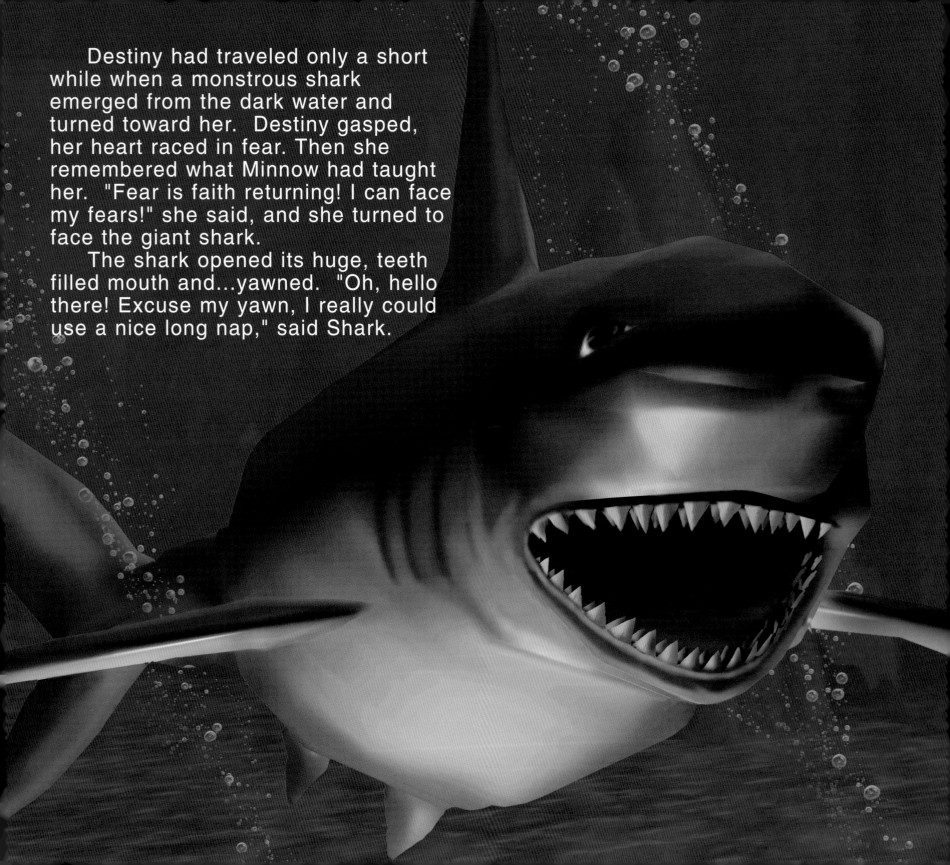

Destiny had traveled only a short while when a monstrous shark emerged from the dark water and turned toward her. Destiny gasped, her heart raced in fear. Then she remembered what Minnow had taught her. "Fear is faith returning! I can face my fears!" she said, and she turned to face the giant shark.

The shark opened its huge, teeth filled mouth and...yawned. "Oh, hello there! Excuse my yawn, I really could use a nice long nap," said Shark.

Destiny felt angry, "You scared me! You didn't have to do that! You ought to be taught a lesson!"

Shark just laughed. "I was just swimming by Dragon. Are you feeling angry at me?"

Destiny just scowled at Shark.

"I'll teach you my trick," said Shark, "When you feel anger at someone else, just say, 'I Choose to Forgive you,' and then take a loving action; do something nice for them. Turn the other cheek."

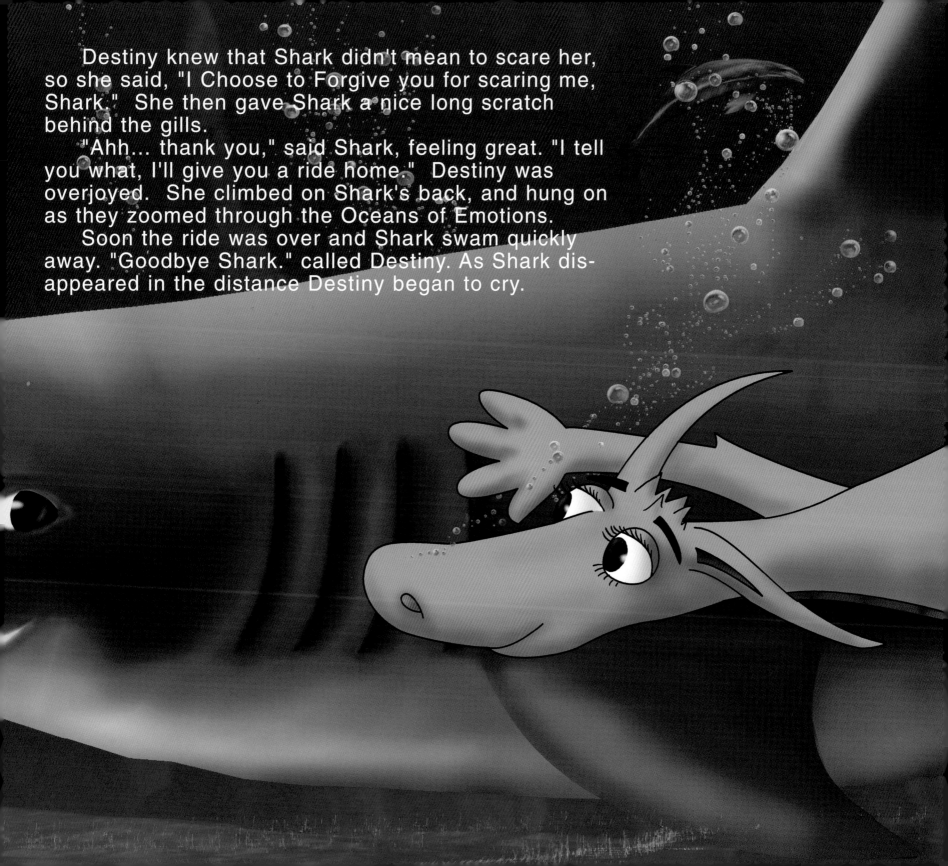

Destiny knew that Shark didn't mean to scare her, so she said, "I Choose to Forgive you for scaring me, Shark." She then gave Shark a nice long scratch behind the gills.

"Ahh... thank you," said Shark, feeling great. "I tell you what, I'll give you a ride home." Destiny was overjoyed. She climbed on Shark's back, and hung on as they zoomed through the Oceans of Emotions.

Soon the ride was over and Shark swam quickly away. "Goodbye Shark." called Destiny. As Shark disappeared in the distance Destiny began to cry.

"Are you feeling hurt?" asked a passing purple Pufferfish, "Do you realize that your hurt and pain is Love Returning."

"What does that mean?" Destiny sniffled.

"Well pain is an emotion that teaches us about life. Whenever you feel pain or hurt it means you are learning an important lesson."

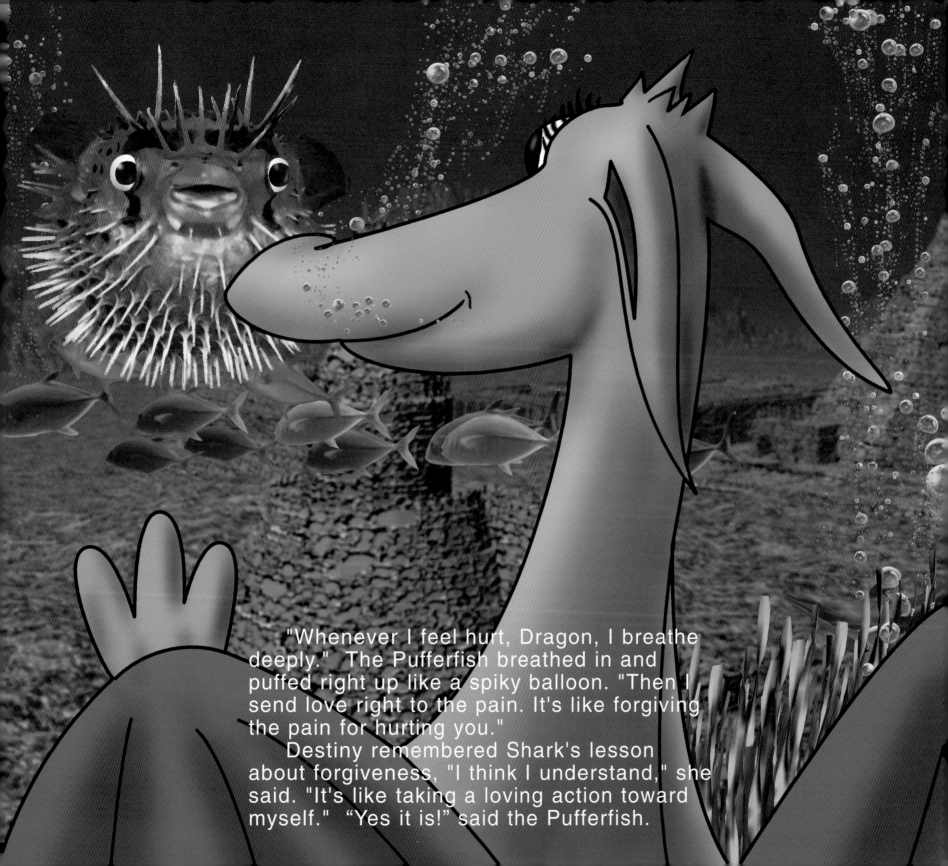

"Whenever I feel hurt, Dragon, I breathe deeply." The Pufferfish breathed in and puffed right up like a spiky balloon. "Then I send love right to the pain. It's like forgiving the pain for hurting you."

Destiny remembered Shark's lesson about forgiveness, "I think I understand," she said. "It's like taking a loving action toward myself." "Yes it is!" said the Pufferfish.

Destiny realized that it was her heart that was aching. She breathed deeply then reached out with as much love as she could find and embraced her aching heart. Quite suddenly all her feelings of being alone melted and she felt the love and friendship of all the creatures who had been helping her to find her way home.

"I feel so wonderfull!" cried Destiny, "I'm glad I fell into the Oceans of Emotions! I have made great friends who have taught me so much about myself. Thank you Pufferfish, you have helped me see how lucky I really am."

Destiny was dancing with delight and happiness when up swam a sleek, powerful dolphin.

"You are feeling Enthusiastic," chittered the dolphin. "My name is Blue. I love to feel Enthusiasm; it feels like Joy, Happiness, Love, Courage, Understanding and Acceptance all rolled into one!!!"

Destiny laughed. "I feel like I can do anything!"

"That's Enthusiasm, too," squeaked Blue. "And I love to be with Enthusiastic people. Hop on my back, let's go for a ride!"

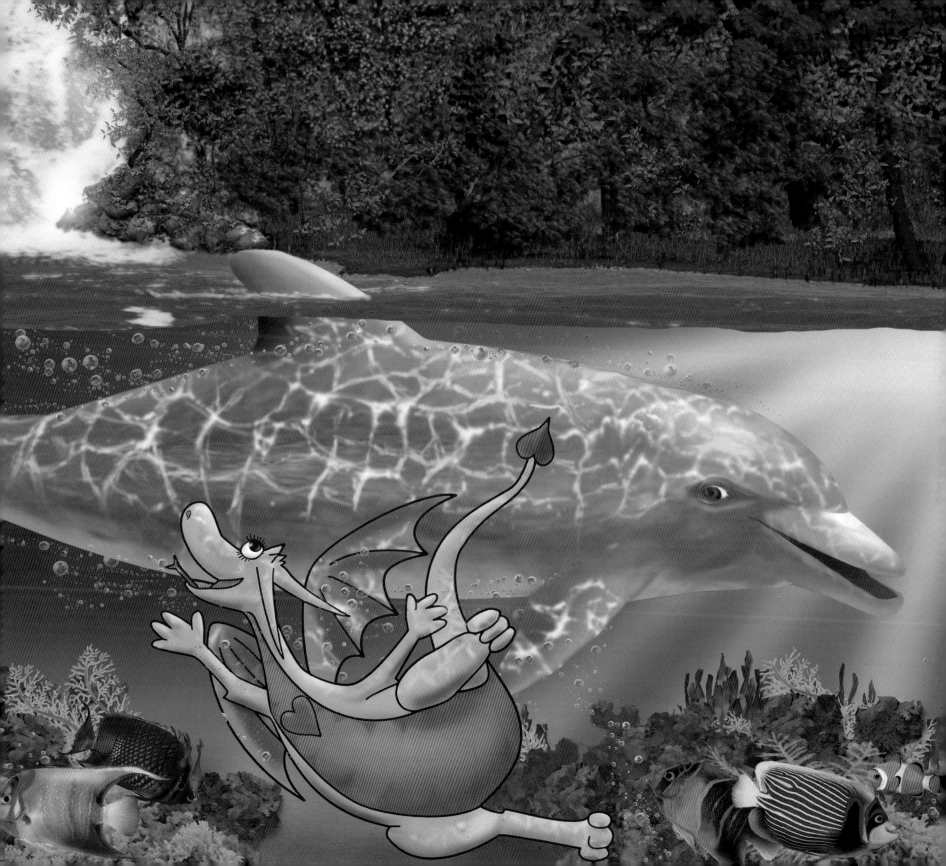

Destiny and Blue played and frolicked in the Oceans of Emotions until the day was over and the sun was setting.

"Here we are," said Destiny when they arrived at her home. "Thank you, Blue."

"You're welcome," squeaked Blue. "Remember Destiny, accept all of your emotions, love all of your feelings. Let them flow through you like an ocean tide. You are the Oceans of Emotions, Destiny and what you say is always what you get!"

Destiny skipped joyfully home. When she saw her Mom and Dad, she felt her emotions rise like an ocean wave. Tears of Joy and relief fell from all their eyes, as they hugged big dragon hugs.

THE END?

PremaNations Mission Statement

To emanate personal integrity, self-responsibility, honesty, leadership and cooperation through our creations. To provide children with educational and entertainment materials that only serve to uplift and empower them through life. To be a force in restoring joy and loving unity to the hearts of families across the Earth.

Text Copyright 1998 by John T. Clark and Nicole K. Clark; Illustrations Copyright 1998 by John T. Clark
All rights reserved. No part of this book may be reproduced or utilized in any form or by any means, electronic or mechanical, including photocopying, recording, scanning or by any information storage and retrieval system, without permission in writing from the publisher.

PremaNations, Inc.
P.O. Box 321447
Cocoa Beach, FL 32932-1447
Printed in Hong Kong
10 9 8 7 6 5 4 3 2

Publishers Cataloging-In-Publication Data
Clark, Nicole
The Oceans of Emotions / John and Nicole Clark ; illustrated by John T. Clark
p. cm.
Summary: Destiny the Dragon is washed into the Oceans of Emotions where she meets undersea creatures who teach her about her emotions and help her find her way home.
ISBN 1-892176-12-2 : $17.95
[1. Emotions- Fiction. 2. The Ocean - Fiction. 3. Conduct of life - Fiction 4.Feelings - Fiction] I. Clark, John T., ill. II. Clark, Nicole K.
PZ7.C6395Em 1998
[E] - dc20   98-96747

Book Ordering Information

Visit your nearest bookstore!

or call us at
PremaNations Publishing:
1-877-DRAGON-4
(1-877-372-4664)

or FAX your order to
1-877-DRAGON-0
(1-877-372-4660)

or order online at our website:
www.premanations.com

or write to:
P.O. Box 321447
Cocoa Beach, FL 32932-1447